Hey Jack! Books

First American Edition 2015
Kane Miller, A Division of EDC Publishing

Text copyright © 2014 Sally Rippin
Illustration copyright © 2014 Stephanie Spartels
First published in Australia in 2014 by Hardie Grant Egmont

For information contact:
Kane Miller, A Division of EDC Publishing
P.O. Box 470663
Tulsa, OK 74147-0663
www.kanemiller.com
www.edcpub.com
www.usbornebooksandmore.com

Library of Congress Control Number: 2014950305

Printed and bound in the United States of America
3 4 5 6 7 8 9 10

ISBN: 978-1-61067-392-1

The Bravest Kid

By Sally Rippin
Illustrated by Stephanie Spartels

Kane Miller
A DIVISION OF EDC PUBLISHING

Feels brave and bold

Exploring hat

Feather monster

Exploring Mood

Chapter One

This is Jack. Today
Jack is in an exploring
mood. He and his best
friend, Billie, are playing
explorers.

They have made a hideout in Billie's backyard. It is made from scraps of wood and tin. From here, they can spy on the **Feather Monsters**.

Billie finds a big plank of wood at the bottom of the woodpile. "Hey," she says. "Let's make a bridge!"

"Good idea!" says Jack.
He helps Billie lift one
end of the plank onto
the roof of their hideout.

They lift the other end
onto the chicken coop.
It makes a very good
bridge.

"Now we can creep up
on the Feather Monsters
without them seeing us!"
Billie says, grinning.
She begins to climb up
onto the plank of wood.

4

"Um," says Jack. "I don't know. It looks dangerous."

"Don't be **silly**!" Billie says. "Look! It doesn't wobble at all!" She pushes the plank of wood.

It doesn't move.

"But still…" Jack says. "What if you fall off? It's a long way to the ground."

His tummy begins to **squeeze** with worry.

Billie rolls her eyes. "The monkey bars at school are much higher than this," she says.

"I know," Jack says. "But…"

"Come on!" says Billie. She climbs up onto the plank of wood and sits waiting for him.

Jack bites the inside of his lip. His heart jumps around. He doesn't want to climb up there.

He wishes she would come down. "I don't want to play this game anymore," he says.

Billie frowns. "You're such a scaredy-cat," she says.

"I'm not!" Jack says.

"You are!" Billie says. "You never want to do anything fun."

"That's not true, Billie!"
Jack says.

"Then prove it!" Billie
says, crossing her arms.

"Fine, I will!" says Jack angrily. He climbs up the side of the hideout. Then he pulls himself up onto the plank next to Billie.

Billie smiles and gives Jack a hug. "See?" she says. "It's not **scary**, is it?"

Jack looks down. It's not very far from the ground. Billie is right. It's not too scary at all.

Chapter Two

"Look at us!" Billie says.

She stands up on the

bridge. Then she holds

her arms out and walks

over to the chicken pen.

"I'm the queen of the world!" she shouts.

Jack grins and stands up too. "And I'm the king of the world!" he yells.

He walks slowly towards
Billie.

Suddenly, a chicken flaps
up towards him. Jack
gets a fright and steps
backward. His foot slips
and he falls off the plank
onto the ground.

"Ow!" he yells. His foot
is twisted up under him.

Billie jumps down beside
him. "Oh no!" she says.
"Are you OK?"

Jack tries to move his
foot. It hurts so much.

15

His tummy squeezes.

But he swallows back
his tears.

He doesn't want Billie
to see him crying.
She might think he isn't
brave.

"Of course I'm OK!" he
says, laughing extra loudly.

Billie looks worried.

"Maybe I should go and get your mom?" she says. "You look pale."

"I'm fine," Jack says.

He frowns. "I think I just twisted my ankle, that's all!" He stands up to show Billie he is OK. Pain **stabs** through his ankle like a knife.

"Here, lean on me," Billie says. "Maybe we should play inside for a bit."

18

Jack leans against Billie.
They hobble back to his
house. Every step makes
Jack's ankle hurt. But he
tries not to let Billie see.

It will stop hurting soon,
he thinks. He hopes he is
right.

That night Jack can't
sleep. His ankle is hurting
so much. He thinks about
telling his mom and dad.
But he doesn't want them
to make a fuss.

It will be better tomorrow,
he thinks.

But the next morning his
ankle is very **swollen**.
It hurts to put his shoe
on. He limps downstairs.
Every step makes his
tummy curl up in pain.

"Are you OK?" says his
mom when she sees him.

"Yes," says Jack. "I just twisted my ankle yesterday. That's all."

Jack's mom kneels down to look at his ankle. "Oh, darling. I think we need to get a doctor to look at that. It looks sore!"

"I'm fine!" says Jack, feeling **cross**. But when his mom touches his foot Jack gasps.

Tears spring into his eyes.

He wipes them away
quickly with his hand.

Jack's mom puts her
hands on her hips.
"Sorry, mister," she says.
"But we are taking you
to a doctor. Right now!"

Jack nods his head.
Finally the big **lump** of
tears in his throat bursts.

It feels good to cry.

His mom gives him
a hug.

"Don't tell Billie," he
says. "She'll think I'm not
brave."

"Don't be silly!" says
Jack's mom. "Billie is
your best friend. She
wouldn't think that."

"But she called me a scaredy-cat," Jack says quietly.

"Well, I'm sure she didn't mean it," says Jack's mom.

"But it wasn't a very nice thing to say. There's nothing wrong with being scared. Sometimes the **bravest** thing you can do is to say that you are scared."

Jack nods his head. He knows his mom is right.

Chapter Three

Jack's mom helps him to the car. They drive to the doctor's office.

There are lots of people in the waiting room.

They wait a long time.
Jack watches the cartoons
on the TV so he doesn't
have to think about his
ankle. It is hurting a lot.

Finally the nurse calls Jack into the doctor's room. Jack tries to stand up, but his ankle hurts so much he **yelps**. Tears fill his eyes.

"Oh dear," says the nurse. She gives Jack some medicine and a little plastic cup of water.

30

"This will help with the pain," she says kindly. She and Jack's mom help him limp into the doctor's office.

Then they help Jack up onto a high bed covered with white paper.

The nurse slips a lollipop into Jack's pocket. "That's for being so brave," she whispers.

"Thank you," Jack says. His voice is high and squeaky.

The doctor has a look
at Jack's ankle. Now it is
very puffy and beginning
to turn purple and blue.

"Hmm. I think your ankle might be broken!" he says.

"Broken?" says Jack. He is surprised.

"Goodness!" says Jack's mom. "You poor thing!" She gives him a cuddle.

"Yes," says the doctor. "See how swollen it is? It must **hurt** a lot."

"Well, I guess it does," Jack says. "I thought it was just twisted, though."

"We'll get you in for an X-ray," says the doctor. "You'll probably need to wear a cast for a few weeks."

Jack grins. A cast! He has never broken a bone before. He can't wait to tell Billie.

That afternoon, Billie
comes to visit Jack after
school. He is sitting in
bed with his foot on
a pillow.

She gives him some comics as a present.

"Wow, a real cast!" Billie says. "Can I sign it?"

"Sure," says Jack **proudly**.

"I can't believe you didn't even cry!" Billie says. "It must have hurt so much."

"It did," Jack says.

"But I didn't want to cry in front of you. I thought you might think I wasn't brave."

"What?" says Billie.

"I think you're super brave! Even though you were scared to come up on the plank with me, you still did it.

That makes you even
braver than me."

"Really?" says Jack.

"Yeah," says Billie.

"And I definitely would
have cried if I broke
my ankle."

"Yeah, but you're a girl,"
Jack says, blushing.
"It's OK for girls to cry."

"That's the **silliest** thing I've ever heard," Billie says. "You are my best friend, Jack. I don't care if you cry."

"Thanks, Billie," says Jack. And even though his ankle still hurts he feels very happy.

The Crazy Cousins
By Sally Rippin

The Scary Solo
By Sally Rippin

The Winning Goal
By Sally Rippin

The Robot Blues
By Sally Rippin

The Worry Monsters
By Sally Rippin

The New Friend
By Sally Rippin

The Worst Sleepover
By Sally Rippin

The Circus Lesson
By Sally Rippin

The Bumpy Ride
By Sally Rippin

The Top Team
By Sally Rippin

The Playground Problem
By Sally Rippin

The Best Party Ever
By Sally Rippin

The Bravest Kid
By Sally Rippin

The Big Adventure
By Sally Rippin

The Toy Sale
By Sally Rippin

Collect them all!